Parents and Caregivers,

Stone Arch Readers are designed to provide enjoyable reading experiences, as well as opportunities to develop vocabulary, literacy skills, and comprehension. Here are a few ways to support your beginning reader:

• Talk with your child about the ideas addressed in the story.

• Discuss each illustration, mentioning the characters, where they are, and what they are doing.

• Read with expression, pointing to each word. You may want to read the whole story through and then revisit parts of the story to ensure that the meanings of words or phrases are understood.

• Talk about why the character did what he or she did and what your child would do in that situation.

• Help your child connect with characters and events in the story.

Remember, reading with your child should be fun, not forced. Each moment spent reading with your child is a priceless investment in his or her literacy life.

Gail Saunders-Smith, Ph.D.

Stone Arch Readers

are published by Stone Arch Books
a Capstone Imprint
1710 Roe Crest Drive
North Mankato, Minnesota 56003
www.capstonepub.com

Library of Congress Cataloging-in-Publication Data
Crow, Melinda Melton.
Rocky and Daisy wash the van / by Melinda Melton Crow; illustrated by Eva Sassin.
p. cm. — (Stone Arch readers: My two dogs)
Summary: Rocky and Daisy "help" their human friend Owen wash the van.
ISBN 978-1-4342-6010-9 (library binding) — ISBN 978-1-4342-6204-2 (pbk.)
1. Dogs—Juvenile fiction. 2. Helping behavior—Juvenile fiction.
[1. Dogs—Fiction. 2. Helpfulness—Fiction.] I. Sassin, Eva, ill. II. Title.
PZ7.C88536Rqr 2013

813.6—dc23   2012047365

Reading Consultants:
Gail Saunders-Smith, Ph.D.
Melinda Melton Crow, M.Ed.
Laurie K. Holland, Media Specialist

Designer: Kristi Carlson

Printed in China by Nordica.
0413/CA21300452
032013
007226NORDF13

Rocky and Daisy
Wash the Van

by **Melinda Melton Crow**
illustrated by **Eva Sassin**

STONE ARCH BOOKS
a capstone imprint

MY TWO DOGS

ROCKY LIKES:

- Chasing squirrels

- Playing with other dogs

- Chewing things

- Running with me when I ride my bike

DAISY LIKES:

- Playing ball

- Listening to stories

- Resting on the furniture

- Eating yummy treats

Rocky and Daisy loved to go
to the dog park. Rocky liked
to run. Daisy fetched the ball.
They always got muddy.

That meant the van got
muddy, too.

"Look at this van!" shouted Mom. There were muddy paw prints inside and dirt on the outside.

Rocky and Daisy looked up at Mom. They did not like the look on Mom's face.

"I'm sorry," said Daisy.

"Me too," said Rocky.

"I will wash the van!" said
Owen. "Rocky and Daisy can
help me. It will be fun."

Mom was not sure how fun it was going to be.

Owen got the vacuum, the
hose, and a bucket. Daisy
found a scrub brush. Rocky was
chewing on a sponge.

"Good luck, Owen," said
Mom. She went into the house.

"Okay," said Owen, "let's vacuum the inside first."

The vacuum was loud. Rocky began barking at it. Daisy ran and hid in the garage.

Mom peeked out the window and frowned.

Owen had to vacuum up the dirt himself.

Owen put some soap into the bucket. Then he put the hose into the bucket and turned on the water.

Rocky stuck his head into the
bucket and pulled out the hose.
Water was spraying everywhere.

"Stop!" said Owen. He tried
to get the hose out of Rocky's
mouth. But he couldn't stop
laughing.

Daisy came running to play
in the water. Mom smiled from
the window.

Finally, Owen got the hose
back from Rocky.

"That was fun!" said Rocky.

"Yes, but now we need to wash the van," said Owen. He sprayed water on the van and began to scrub.

The dogs helped, too. Rocky
scrubbed the front tires with the
brush. Daisy scrubbed the back
tires with the sponge.

"Yuck," said Daisy. "I don't like soap."

Rocky helped Owen rinse the
van with water. They dried it
and cleaned the windows.

Then they sat and looked at
the clean van.

"It looks perfect," said Daisy,
smiling.

"I'm hot," said Rocky. "Can we play in the water again?"

"Yes!" said Owen. "I'll give you a bath too!"

He used the sponge to scrub
Rocky and Daisy. Then he used
the hose to rinse them off.

Mom brought out towels for
Rocky and Daisy.

"Wow, a clean van AND clean dogs," she said. "Thank you!"

"You're welcome," said Owen.
"I knew we could do it."

Mom smiled.

Rocky and Daisy looked up at Mom again. They liked the look on Mom's face now!

THE END

STORY WORDS

fetched	bucket	sponge
vacuum	scrub	rinse

Total Word Count: 410

READ MORE
ROCKY AND DAISY ADVENTURES!